Dedicated To You

Chapter 1

The old grey headed preacher poured out three tiny drops of sand from those big hands of his, and I carefully watched as they silently fell six feet down till they finally touched the bottom of the hole. I did not want to believe it. Everyone was crying, so I came closer, looked deep down the hole, and in my tears, I laughed, I felt hands come hold me from my back saying it was ok.

I knew it was not ok, I cursed God, I cursed Kevin, I missed him. What on earth was I going to do without him?

At the point when the preacher said, may his soul rest in peace; I felt the world had come to a standstill. Memories of Kevin and I ran through my mind, the good, the bad, and the ugly,

What about Vanessa? What was going to happen to her? I wondered what was running through her mind too. I could not afford to talk to her at that moment; I could see her die slowly in her tears. For her it was the end of the world.

As much as I hated it but could do nothing about it, in the crowd, she walked towards me, looked at me on the face like it was her last moment on earth and then she said “He is gone forever”

I could see more tears fall down her lovely cheeks, and then she embraced me, and cried on my shoulders, I could not bear it too, so together with her I cried. But in my cry, I told her it was ok, and she told me I was lying.

“Have you been able to talk to Tracy?” she asked. Tracy had not been able to get out of that room for more than four hours; she refused to witness the burial. It might have been hard for Vanessa and I, but we all knew it was worse for Tracy. We wondered how she was going to cope with it. All she had was little Tatiana, the baby was just two months old, so she knew not of what was going on. How on earth was I going to face Tracy?

So Vanessa and I walked to the room. The door was open, and we could see Tracy sitting on the chair by the preachers study table. As Vanessa walked in, Tracy looked up and saw her, and cried again as if she had just heard the news that her husband was dead. She tried to speak out but words refused to come out of her mouth. She looked at me, then looked at the baby,

"What are we going to do without him? Just look at her, she does not even know what is happening, Tatiana is fatherless" She cried,

I could not bear talking any longer because I never wanted to cry again, so I came closer, and though it killed me inside, I picked up the baby from Tracy's hands and told Vanessa to help Tracy out. "You are not going to stay in the preachers study rooms for ever, let us go home" so I told her and walked out with the baby and they slowly followed us outside.

The others were already waiting for us and some had already gone ahead. I opened the car door and waited for Vanessa and Tracy to get in. I handed the baby over to Vanessa, put on my seat belt and started to slowly drive home.

Chapter 2

Kevin and I had been best friends even before we were born. His mother was my mother's best friend. I was just two months older than him though he looked taller and more muscular. When we were kids we played around like fools, we shared secretes together, we talked about what we wanted to become. We enjoyed being with each other, and we shared almost everything in common.

We climbed hills and trees together; we went to the movies together. We studied together. We did everything in the name of together.

He was more than just my best friend; he was like a brother to me. Though sometimes we would ague and fight over stupid things, we always reconciled and life would continue.

In secondary school, we met Tracy, and since then she has been a very good companion to us. She is a very gentle and beautiful girl, tall with long black hair, and a very supernaturally good character. Honestly I think she is an angel sent from above.

She never complains about anything, she always wears a smile on her face, never uses offending words, and best of all she was Vanessa's best Friend.

Ok, Kevin had a problem with that. Vanessa was Kevin's only junior sister; he had no other brother or sister so he very much cherished her. Most of the time Tracy would want Vanessa to hang around with us, but Kevin would always reject, he was so conservative of her but with time he got used to Vanessa being around us.

Just like Tracy, Vanessa was an angel, she had white well shaped teeth, and every time she smiled, it was like the whole world was rejoicing. She knew how to take care of herself, and most beautifully she knew how to cook well and how to handle all sorts of situations.

We lived life to the fullest and honestly I do not regret a thing.

It was fun. Friends called us the fantastic four. Everyone envied us in school. We walked, talked, studied and played together. We all were very intelligent, the girls were exceptionally beautiful and the boys tall, muscular, funny and sexy.

Every single guy in school wanted to be Kevin and I, and all the girls wanted to hook up with us. It was not our fault for being so attractive. We enjoyed that gift of nature. And we always thanked God for it.

And Before I forget my own name is Taku Jackson, Kevin's best friend and a guy of high moral value and great life principles. Unlike Kevin who dreamed to work for the UN, I had always dreamed to be rich famous and influential and I had planned to achieve my goals through becoming a business man.

In high school we hooked up with many girls, rejected some, and had fun. Vanessa and Tracy were of great help to us because they knew the girls in school and could tell us which was a good one and who was a bad one.

Finally we went to the university. We left Vanessa and Tracy back. We were two years ahead of them in school, but that did not separate us at all. The university was still in the same town, and we left home to school everyday. When we returned from school we would still be together. And during vacations we spent much time together and sometimes we would invite our girlfriends and boyfriends over.

In high school, Vanessa found Felix and they seemed happy together, Tracy Found Lionel and they often invited them over. We were all very happy with it. Sometimes things went wrong but we'll always put them back in order.

CHAPTER 3

Two years later, Vanessa and Tracy graduated too from high school and came over to the university. As every senior would do, Kevin and I always protected Vanessa and Tracy from all the wild hungry beasts in the university who were always looking for someone to assault.

I'm talking about the senior boys; you know they are always crazy over freshmen. We protected them like a dog will do its puppies.

But then in the university, something strange started to happen, Kevin and Tracy became closer than ever, they always complemented each other, and often Kevin would remind me that Tracy looked more beautiful than ever, and I would accept, because it was true, but what I never imagined, was the fact that Kevin could fall for Tracy.

Tracy was like a buddy to us, she was a friend, and she knew us way too much for anyone of us to try to date her. Worst of all she was Kevin's junior sister's best friend. How was Vanessa going to feel, if she knew Kevin was in love with Tracy.

It is not a lie that she had become very beautiful and irresistible. And finally the day came when Kevin officially told me that he was falling for Tracy. We chatted over it and then decided that Kevin should let her know.

We wondered how she was going to react towards it, but yet Kevin was ready to give it a try. I had no idea if Vanessa had suspected that Kevin had fallen for Tracy, so I decided to talk to Vanessa.

One day we went out to the fields to play, Vanessa and I sat down and watched Kevin and Tracy run around like fools, and so to get Vanessa's opinion, I said "I think those two do better together" and Vanessa replied "Yeah, Looks like they are in love" "I thought I was the only one that was noticing it" I said "Just take a look at them, they smile together, laugh at each others jokes, look into each others eyes, they always look happy together" Vanessa said, then we looked over at them, Kevin saw us looking and waved his hands at us and asked us to come over but before we could even shake our heads or wave our hands to reject, Tracy had run fast and held him by the waist and they both fell and rolled on the green grass like a newly wedded couple on honeymoon.

We could no longer see them, they were lost in the grass for a while and we wondered what had happened. Then we saw Tracy stand up and run towards us, I could not really tell if she seemed happy or sad, from afar, but then as she came closer, Kevin too stood up and watched her run towards us but said or did nothing.

From the way Tracy was running, I suspected that something bad had happened. Finally Tracy arrived at the spot where Vanessa and I were seated, and picked up her bag angrily, said nothing and walked away. Vanessa decided to run after her and I decided to walk towards Kevin to hear what had happened.

Kevin stood quiet for some time then finally told me as though he was crying. "I kissed her" and then I told him "I understand, let's just go home". While we walked home, Kevin kept on asking me questions like; do you think she will accept me? Do you think she hates me for kissing her? And I kept telling him that I did not know but that I prayed that things should work out well for them.

"She did not resist when I was kissing her, she kissed me like she loved me. It was just after the kiss that she left without saying a word." Kevin said and I said we could just wait and see. I called Vanessa to find out about Tracy and what was going on, and she said Tracy had refused to utter a word to her. And that she did not know what to do. So I asked Kevin that we go over to Tracy's to see her.

CHAPTER 4

After a couple of resists by Kevin and insists by me, I finally convinced him that we go there. He put on his black jacket and we left for Tracy's. In no time, we had arrived, I knocked at the door and Vanessa came over and opened it. We entered and saw Tracy seating on the couch. Then I signaled Vanessa and we excused both of them, Vanessa and I walked out the living room. We stood by the door and spied through the glass to see what would happen.

Kevin stood speechless for a moments, then I saw him walk towards Vanessa, held her by the hand, and she looked him straight in the eyes "I'm sorry for kissing you" he said "I just cant do without you, I love you and am willing to climb the highest mountain just to make you mine" then still holding her hand, he sat on the couch, and continued to tell her how much he loved her, then all of a sudden we saw their faces come closer and closer, and we held our hands tight together outside praying that they kiss and they did.

It was a rail way road kiss, I heard Tracy tell him "I love you too" and they looked at each other and kissed again. Then of a sudden they started laughing. Vanessa and I saw that as a good sign and then opened the door and entered.

Then Vanessa said "we saw that, my best friend and my brother, O am touched" then she embraced them and they laughed together. They asked me to come join them but I refused and said I preferred the view.

Chapter 5

Life became so sweet with Kevin and Tracy. I was extremely happy for them, and sometimes I even got jealous because the two of them were very good together. I had to accept the fact that Kevin would stop spending much of his time with me, and it was same for Vanessa.

When the four of us walked together, the two of them always seemed happier, and would always make Vanessa and I walk a little bit behind them, we were sometimes bored by their love, if not always.

Vanessa's boyfriend, Felix had gone to a different state University, but often returned to Yaoundé for weekends and vacations. And when ever he came over, I was always lonely because Kevin would spend almost all his time with Tracy and Vanessa would do same with Felix.

Though I was lonely, I coped with it. I would play video games, and watch movies, and dated girls online. Sometimes, we all would go to the movies together. But that would be boring for me because of them. When ever Felix returned to school,

Vanessa became my friend again, and life would be a little better.

Sometimes when the four of us walked together, they'll advice me to get a girlfriend. I would often tell them that I had not found the girl that I loved. And I was not really willing to have a serious relationship with just any girl. But sometimes it became unbearable, so I decided to take their advice and find myself a girlfriend.

I made a list and I called it the magic list. It had the names of some of the sexiest and most beautiful girls on campus. I was in search of a relationship that could last for ever. Like happily ever after. I wanted a girl who would know me by heart, who would understand me and who would respect me.

I wanted a girl who had plans for the future, and last but not least. I needed a girl who shared the same passions for music and movies like me. And not to forget, a girl who had morals and good principles. If Vanessa was not my best friend's junior sister, or was not going out with Felix, or did not know me way too much, she would have been the best partner

Vacations were over and Felix left, So Vanessa helped me to review my magic list. Kevin and Tracy were too busy to be concerned about that. Vanessa and I had fun in reviewing the girls and trying them out. And we got to get to know each other even better because we spent more time together than ever.

Chapter 6

First on the magic list was Stella. Stella was a living angel; she has an irresistible charm, sexy wide eyes and a smile that never faded away. But I had a problem with Stella. I felt she was too good for me. In fact I felt I was not good enough for her and that she deserved a better guy, so I cut her off the list.

Then second was, Christy, Just like the name she was a full time Christian, sexy and romantic too, I met her and wooed her, but in the long run I could not bear her nagging attitude. So I cut her off the list. I really miss her good cooking and passion for sharing ideas.

Third was Charlotte, I had known her since secondary school. And she had all the qualities I wanted, but something did not seem to go on well with us. Was it the Manish perfume she used, or the fact that she was growing fat or what, I could not really tell, but I cut her off the list?

Then next was Olivia. She had all the magic list qualities and she is the sexiest girl I have ever seen, but it seems like she never wanted a serious relationship, she just wanted to have fun and trust me I was not in for that, so I dropped her off the list but I continued to see her because I enjoyed having fun with her. And I kept on hoping someday she would think about taking the relationship to another level but it did not work. So I stopped seeing her.

Last was Agnes. She too was beautiful, sexy, intelligent, romantic and principled. We fooled around for about a month, crazily like a newly wedded couple but we never knew the force that bonded us was that of brotherly love. O yes you hear me right, I found out she was a relative. Well not very close but you know how Africa is, even your great grand mothers uncles, wife's Anti's Cousins, Grand Children, are forbidden. So we decided to stop, seeing each other. But we remained being friends and we became even closer than ever.

All this passed so fast, and once again, Vanessa and I were seated. "I wish I could help you" she said to me. "Do not bother Vanessa, am a grown up boy, I will make it through." So I replied but God knows I was dying inside.

It was already my last year in the university. One day Kevin called all of us over to their house, and told us he was going to Paris for a field trip and that he was going to spend two months there. He asked me to take good care of Tracy and Vanessa for him, and told them to always come to me when ever they needed anything. "Of course you do not need to tell me all that, what are friends for, you are my best friend for Gods sake, and you are like a brother to me and Vanessa is like a junior sister" I promised him I was going to be there for them.

Before we knew it, we had gone to see him off at the airport, and the last words he said to me where "Do not let any guy still my girl, and do not let any fool break my sisters heart. They are all I have" I laughed and wished him a save journey and the three of us returned. As usual, Tracy and Vanessa stayed together, but this time Kevin was gone, and I was alone. I wondered how I was going to stay alone in that house for that time, but I had no choice. After all, someday I was going to start living alone.

Chapter 7

Three months is a very long time and many things could change.

Vanessa, Tracy and I spent most of the time together. I got to know them better. We played and went to the movies. Life was very beautiful until, I started to notice something very unusual.

I was beginning to fall for Vanessa. I became jealous anytime a boy greeted her, I got lost in her smiles and when she walked I admired her. I tried to resist but it was so difficult. Sometimes I would just feel guilty; I was left to guide and protect her and instead I was falling for her.

When the feelings became unbearable, I decided to talk to Tracy about it. I told Tracy that I had been observing Vanessa and to me it looked like I was beginning to fall for her and I also thought she liked me too.

Then Tracy told me maybe I was getting it wrong, that Vanessa was just trying to be a friend and that all the smiles she threw at me were just a normal thing and even worse of all she said that I was not her type. "How could you even be thinking about that? She is your best friend's sister. How do you think Kevin is going to feel if he found out that instead of taking care of his sister you are falling for her"

She also reminded me about Vanessa's boyfriend Felix who already had his degree, and began working at a bank and that they were planning on getting married as soon as Vanessa completed her education. But I did not consider Felix as a threat because I knew two years was a very long time and anything could happen.

I thanked Tracy for the advice and begged her not to tell anybody about it, and she accepted. But deep inside I was not satisfied. I was in love and would not breathe till I had gotten her.

Zillions of thoughts ran through my brain. Kevin and I had been best friends even before we were born and I remember he often said if any of his friends wooed his sister, he was going to kill him. I was not yet ready to destroy our friendship; but neither was I willing to let my love go.

Funny enough I had not even told her that I loved her, I did not know if she would love me back, or if she would accept me, and worst of all she had a boyfriend and I knew she knew that I knew about him.

So now you see how complicated it is. How would I begin, what would I say, what if she says we are already friends, what if I tell her and she hates me for it. I spent more than a month wondering over it. Tracy and Vanessa would come over to my place and life still continued as usual, Tracy never told Vanessa about our chat and whenever three of us were together, though I found it hard to do, I would look at Tracy just as a sister.

Time passed and the second semester break came. It was our first vacation without Kevin, Felix came over and I got to meet him, once or twice in the company of Vanessa of course and she introduced me as a friend but I never really associated with him except for greetings.

It was difficult for me to know him or want to associate with him, but I tried my best till the two week vacation was over.

I felt very guilty not letting Vanessa know that I loved her, but I also thought of how guilty I would be if she rejected me. So in my best interest, I remained neutral.

CHAPTER 8

Felix went back to Douala where he worked, and life started all over again, but this time around, strange things began to happen. Sometimes I closed my eyes but I could not sleep, I kept wondering how I was going to do to get her to love me and to accept me.

This time around I never cared about what Kevin was going to think. The love was consuming me like wild fire in a dry forest. I was willing to face the consequences of my actions. Though sometimes I would laugh at myself and wonder how I of all people could fall for a girl like Vanessa and why it would be this time in life.

Why had I not fallen in love with her earlier?

All the same, I thanked God for the gift of love, and I prayed and wished she was going to love me back. Even if it were to last just for a moment. I was willing to give up everything for her. Honestly Tracy was the love of my life and I was willing to spend the rest of my life with her.

I got lost in her charms, I got lost in her smiles. I got lost in her voice, and I understood why people would have to die for love.

CHAPTER 9

A few days after Felix had returned to Douala, An idea came to my mind, like lightening on a rainy day. I had figured out a plan. I called it the magic plan. I did not really know what the plan was all about, but I was not going to tell Vanessa that I loved her, just then. I was going to make her love and want me, till it reaches a point where she would not be able to hide her feelings anymore, and then I would ask her out.

But how would I make her love me? How would I make her look at me and would not see but a brother or just a normal friend? All this thoughts kept on hunting me like a wild lion searching for a prey, but I was determined to be strong, for once in my life I was determined to be man.

I made sure anytime I spoke to her, I was romantic, I would always hold her hand, look her straight and direct in the eyes. All the times, I sounded sincere in my speech, and talked about my future in such a way that would make her love to be a part of it.

I would talk about how I was going to love my wife and children and how we would live happily ever after, and because she had same points of view like me she always felt in love with me and my ideas,

I became more very gentle and caring towards her. And I enjoyed being with her.

CHAPTER 10

Then I started noticing results, when I acted romantic, she would want to come closer, hold my hand, smile at me, laugh at my jokes, but when ever I noticed she was coming to close, I went away, but continued to act romantic to make her want me more and more.

Tracy discovered what I wanted to do and got angry with me, and told me she was not going to support my evil intentions and that I was going to face the wrath of Kevin alone.

I would have gotten scared, but I did not, I had made the choice, and I was willing to face the consequences, I tried to explain to Tracy that I honestly and truly loved Vanessa, but she did not understand. Or maybe did not want to.

So I decided to stop wasting my precious energy trying to convince Tracy. And by the way, with time, my magic plan was giving positive results and I was happy, who was Tracy to make me sad. Love takes over your heart and brain so fast you can not even notice. It eats you up, yet you want it more, it has the power to heal and the power to destroy. It is a blessing and a curse at the same time. The funniest thing about love is that it makes even the most uncourageous people stand up with more faith and nerve than ever,

CHAPTER 11

I took the bold step, I was ready to tell her, but I told no body, not even Tracy, I was not very sure if she would accept or reject because all those signs could still mean nothing. I was ready to stop being a coward, but I would have been a double coward if I told the whole world that I loved Vanessa, but then she rejects me.

So one faithful Friday morning, lying in my couch and watching the 7:30 news, I picked up my mobile phone, stared at it for a moment as if it were Vanessa and then I slowly punched one digit after another and dialed her phone number;

She answered, and I wondered around the bush for a moment before I finally told her I had something important to tell her and that anytime she would be free, she let me know.

She told me that, that evening she would have some minutes to spare. And I was ok with it, so I told her I was going to pass pick her up at six thirty in the evening for supper at the Chinese restaurant.

The whole day I panicked, cleaned up, dressed up, I tried like some ten different outfits, and finally selected that rock star jacket that no girl could resist.

I used to use that jacket when ever I wanted to woo a girl in school. It was my good luck charm. I dressed up before five o'clock in the evening, and gently sat on the couch, anxiously waiting for time to pass so fast. Every second seemed like a year, I was becoming too desperate for my liking. I tried a glass of wine, but it did me no good. Tried video games but they did not seem to make time pass faster, I tried to sleep, but it was worse, so I just walked around the house from room to room, touching cups and spoons in the kitchen for no good reason

Then all of a sudden, I heard that song play on my phone

"You are the girl of my dreams

The reason I am alive

You are fruit I desire

You are the only thing that gives me joy

Every single day

I think of you

Thoughts of you are always fresh

Fresh in my mind like a kiss on a lip

I wish to spend the rest of my life with you"

That was my ring tone, I loved it very much. It was like the musician sang the song just for me. It was Vanessa calling.

I waited for a moment, then I picked up and answered and she said she was ready and that I could come pick her up, so not to sound desperate I asked her to give me some time.

I sat down on my bed doing nothing for about fifteen minute before I took off. When I arrived at her door and knocked, she opened, and smiled and honestly she looked gorgeous, she wore a sexy black gown which fitted with the color of her hair and matched with her handbag and shoes. In my astonishment, I said to her "you look amazing" and she said "thank you"

Like every gentle man with principles, I apologized for being late and once again I complemented her dressing and hair style something I had not done since I started the magic plan, formerly no matter how nice her hair or dress was I just said she looked ok and I saw a bigger smile than ever, on her face, it made me feel lucky, and my heart skipped a beat.

I took her by the hand, and let her into my car. She kept on smiling all through, till we entered the splendid Chinese restaurant, I knew it was her favorite spot in town. We were shown to our table where we sat and ordered and were served, and we ate.

She looked extremely happy, then came the wine, and just before she sipped her first, I called her name softly surely but steadily, 'Vanessa" and she looked up, our eyes met and it cut through my heart like a sharp razor , she had never looked this beautiful before, I have never felt this much in love before,

Millions of thoughts ran through my mind, but as a guy with principles, I acted like nothing had happened. I knew she had been waiting anxiously to hear what I wanted to say and I do not know what she had in mind that I wanted to say.

CHAPTER 12

I too was a very unpredictable guy; she knew I could just have wanted to go out and have a drink with her just for fun. While we ate she asked me over and over again what I wanted to say but I asked her to finish eating. Well now was the time, I sent my hand, and held hers, looked into her eyes and found myself gradually dying for her and in my most romantic and gentle way ever, I told her

"I know you have been my friend for a long time now and your brother too is my best friend, we have been through a lot together and I have known you ever since. I know you, and I think you are a good person, I have been observing you and I think you are one of the best friends I have ever had, I have a problem that has seriously been killing me inside and I have not yet told anybody about it and I would love to share it with you."

She looked so surprised and concerned, her face was full of wonder, then I heard her say "you know am always there for you, just voice it out" then I said "you know I have been looking for a girlfriend right?" she nodded her head with some kind of serious attention to me, then I said " you know very much the criteria I always want for a girl and especially that I want a relationship that can last and that I am not into jokes right?" and she said "yes I do", Then I told her I had searched and I had found the girl I was looking for and I was wishing we could be able to spend the rest of our life together, she of a sudden stopped the serenity scene and became so stupidly excited "I am happy for you, who is she, who is she?" I told her to clam down and seat down and she did, and I said "I know this may look funny or surprising or maybe even crazy but actually the girl I found is you."

We were both silent for a moment, no one spoke to each other, I looked up at her sunshine eyes and put my head down and she too would do same, I decided to fix my eyes directly on her face, then I said " Please Vanessa say something" then she softly confusingly asked " What do you want me to say" " all I want to do is to love and treat you right" I replied, then the next thing she said was "you know Kevin would kill you if he heard about this right? You know about Felix right?" and I slowly but reluctantly answered "yes I know, but trust me I have considered all that before taking this great step" then she said "Then why would you be asking me this type of a thing. It is not fair. You know very well that even if I loved you, it will not be possible for us to be together, you are like a brother to me"

At that moment I felt like the whole world was coming to an end, all my hopes died, I could feel every single blood cell dry off my bones, and then she said " I am going to pretend that none of this ever happened, and we will continue to be the normal friends we have always been" I knew she was serious so I never wanted to get her on her nerves or worse to let her walk out on me in a public place, so I said, " Vanessa I understand how you feel, but" "please stop it" she said a little loud and angry and behaved as if she wanted to stand up and walk away so I calmed down and softly said " I just want you to think about it" then she said there's nothing to think about, "there's no way we can ever be together. Please I like it the way we are, do not spoil things" so I said ok I understand lets finish our drinks.

And trying be gentle we emptied our glasses and smiled and walked out like nothing had happened, I took her to her home, said goodbye by the door and asked her to sleep well. And then quietly I walked away with a gallon of tears flowing from my heart.

CHAPTER 13

At last I arrived at my house, and to my greatest surprise, Kevin had returned and was resting on the couch. He had my spare keys and that's how he got in. at a first glance at him, I wondered how fast three months had passed, I watched him lay in the couch and I wondered what I was going to tell him when he asked where I was coming from, but then he was not my father, somewhere inside me I felt I should be honest with him, but I was not ready to spoil his first day back.

So I walked towards the couch and tapped his shoulder till he got up. In his sleepy nature, he looked at me and first thing he said was, that he was sorry for not information us that he was coming, he said he wanted it to be a surprise.

He wanted us to talk too much that night, but I was not in the mood, I was just returning from where I had received a heart punch from his junior sister, I tried to hide the bulk of sorrow that piled in my heart which indeed was so heavy for me to bear. And in my most possible gentle way, I convinced him that he had traveled from so far, and that he needed a rest and that we were going to talk the next morning. But deep down in my heart I knew I was the one that needed a rest

I thought I was just going to fall in bed, close my eyes and sleep like a new born baby, but that was not the case. I found it very hard to sleep that night, pictures of how she closed me up kept passing through my eyes into my brain and then found their way deep down into my heart, where they caused a burning desire for me to want to die, and took away every bit of my will to sleep.

I felt like someone special had died, I felt like I was death. I thought about how I was going to spend my life without a partner or with someone I did not love, and those thoughts brought me nothing but sorrow and a gallon of tears in my soul.

As if the pain in my heart was not enough, morning refused to come. I prayed and wondered my eyes around the room. I felt like I was empty, I was ashamed of myself. I felt like all hopes were lost. And that's how funny life is. Just a small obstacle and we fill like the world has come to an end.

CHAPTER 14

Before Kevin woke up that morning, I was already up and had prepared breakfast. I even cleaned the sitting and bedrooms. I called Tracy and told her I had a surprise for them and that she should not fail to bring Vanessa along.

While we ate, I told him I had asked Vanessa and Tracy to come over and that they would arrive at any moment. I still felt bad deep down inside but I was willing to hide and die in my sorrow.

Then we heard a knock on the door and we knew it was them, Kevin rushed and hid himself in the room and I walked towards the door to open it. I peeped through the peep hole and noticed that the two of them were there and I felt a bit relieved. I was scared that Vanessa was not going to come, especially after last nights events. I thought she was going to hate me for asking her out.

So then, I opened the door. Tracy was first so I embraced her and kissed her by the cheek, and let her inn. She immediately started to ask loud and wonder around the room asking and looking for the surprise I told her I was keeping.

"Do not be so desperate" I shouted at her, then I turned to Vanessa still standing by the door, I looked at her and she looked at me and none of us said anything to each other, then I shifted and paved the way for her to walk in and she did.

She did not show any signs of being happy or sad, but as for me I had decided to put up a smiling face no matter what.

Vanessa entered and quietly sad down on the couch, then I called out for Tracy and she came out of the kitchen where she had already landed on a loaf of bread, and was seriously digesting it. I asked her to sit down by Tracy, and I could see them wonder what kind of surprise I was going to bring out. Then I asked them to close their eyes and they did, then Kevin slowly came out of the room and stood in front of the TV, then I asked them to open their eyes

They both skipped from the chair like cats and landed on Kevin like playing puppies. And then they all fell down on the floor. The atmosphere was like Christmas or some family reunion. Standing and smiling at the corner, I could see them laugh and smile and ask millions of questions at a time. The joy lasted a moment and finally they all settled down and began to ask questions and got replies in order.

I did not want to be noticed in the corner so I walked to the kitchen and picked up some wine and juice for refreshment. Then we all sat by Kevin and heard him tell his beautiful stories about his journey and experiences in Europe. He said he loved the place and intended to settle there. Tracy loved the idea, though I mocked at it, saying there was no place as sweet as home.

While we chatted I observed Vanessa and prayed she did not mention anything about the previous night, and luckily she did not. Then I heard Kevin ask Vanessa about Felix. She looked like she did not want to respond but then she finally said they were all fine, and that he even came over for holidays.

Kevin presented the gifts he brought us from Paris and we loved them. He brought Tracy a sexy red carpet gown with handbag, and a laptop for Vanessa, then to me he gave a hand made square well designed and decorated wooden frame which on it was written in French the words "Ensembles pour tourjours" which in English meant "Together Forever" he read it loud to me and told me this was a symbol of our friendship. I embraced him and tears of joy dropped from my eyes.

The chit chat continued for about two hours, and then we moved on to a bar not far from school where we shared drinks with other friends.

CHAPTER 15

While we drank, my mind was completely somewhere else. I was thinking about the gift Kevin had given me, and how he would feel if he realized that I was in love with his junior sister. I was so much drunk in my thoughts that I almost missed one of the most important moments of my best friend's life.

I heard a deep silence in the bar, so I looked up. Everyone was sited and all were looking towards Kevin who stood up alone, and looked fresher than milk on Sunday morning. For once in my life I said Europe was a good place.

Kevin stood silent for a moment, then reached his hands into his pocket, turned his back to the people, brought out something from his pocket, behaved as if he were opening it and then turned back to face us and said,

"I don't know what to say

Today am happy

But I want to be happier

And luckily enough for me, I have found the secrete which will make me to be the happiest man on earth.

Then he looked at where I sat, and I thought he was looking at me. Everybody looked in my direction, and I felt somewhat embarrassed, but then I heard him loudly say

"Atika Tracy, I will be very pleased if you make me the happiest man on earth by accepting this precious ring"

I heard the crowd mummer in amazement, and all eyes fell back at my direction and only just then did I understand that Tracy was sited besides me. I felt relieved. And I too turned to look towards her.

She stood up, and walked towards him and we all were in silence. Then she reached where he stood and looked him in the eyes, embraced him and gave her hand, and then I saw him put the sparkling ring into her fingers. It was amazing, I felt like I was the one giving the ring. They kissed and the crowd cheered and clapped, it was like the ambiance had just started all over again, more drinks and more drunken talk.

Vanessa Joined Kevin and Tracy on stage, and embraced them, and so did I. I congratulated them and we all happily returned to our sits.

That night Tracy came over and spent the night at our place with Kevin in his room. And the next day she and Vanessa packed her things and officially Tracy moved over to our house. She really seemed happy and so was Kevin. It was like they had just newly fallen in love. Honestly I envied them. Watching them play like kids in the same house with me. They looked as beautiful as my new car which they very much loved by the way.

CHAPTER 16

Since Tracy was now living with us, Vanessa was alone and as such often came over to visit Tracy, but never ever mentioned anything about us to Kevin or Tracy till one evening she came over, I was not at home, but Tracy and her fiancé were. I opened the door and noticed that the environment was not as funky as was the case in the previous days. So I walked closer to them, and just then I saw Kevin look at me with those eyes, he looked like he was going to kill somebody, then I saw Vanessa lie on Tracy's labs and I heard her cry and could see Tracy trying to console her.

I started to wonder if Vanessa had told them about us, but then I was not so sure. If she had done so, Kevin would have already torn me into pieces. So I asked out silently to Kevin, "what's up with her" Kevin looked at me again like he was looking at some devil and then he picked up a paper from the table with hand written text and handed it over to me without saying a word.

I took it from his hand, but was scared to look into it or to read it, then Kevin urged me with his head and quietly said "read it". So I turned it over, and looked at it. It was a letter, and my eyes immediately fell on the address line which indicated Douala as the writing town.

I immediately thought it was from Felix, but then I looked at the bottom line which was signed Angela. I got a little bit confused, so I asked Kevin again and again, "What is this" and he quietly told me just to read it. By this time I felt a little bit free because I knew Vanessa had not sold me out yet. But deep down I knew it was just a matter of time for my anus to be showed in public. Here is what the letter said.

Dearest Vanessa,

My name is Angela. I have heard a lot about you from my girlfriends and from Felix. And I'm very sure you are a very good and understanding person so I pray you take in the best way possible, this saddening message I'm about to tell you

Felix and I have been friends ever since secondary school. And I've always stood by him where and when ever necessary.

I am so sorry to inform you that Felix and I have gotten married. I just wanted to inform you before you hear it from a different person. I know about the affair you had with my husband but it is not my fault he could not keep away his stupid desires when he crawled over me and now am pregnant.

I wish you the best in life and hope you find a new man soon.

Best regards

Angela

I quietly kept the letter on the table and stood quiet for some time, it was indeed a disheartening letter. I felt very sad for Vanessa but then somewhere in my brain I felt happy because this had given me a better chance. But then in harmony with the others, I wore a gloomy face. Then I signaled Kevin to join me outside and together we walked outside.

CHAPTER 17

We stood quiet for a moment then he said

"I knew it, I knew that guy was fake, I wondered how a man of his age would be able to love a child like Vanessa, he could not even be able to keep his thing in his pants, I swear this is the last heartbreak my junior sister will ever have, if anybody ever breaks her heart again, I will personally tear him into pieces"

"Personally cut him into pieces", those words cut through my heart like a sharp razor.

I told him not to be so quick at drawing conclusions and then asked him if anybody had called Felix to verify if what Angela claimed was true. He said Vanessa had done so and all Felix said was that he was sorry. And that it was true that he was married and was expecting a baby.

We left the ladies to deal with the problem for sometime then Tracy came out and asked me to go try calm Vanessa down. She said that she had tried to no avail. I asked Tracy and Kevin to wait outside and then I moved in alone.

I sat down besides her and saw how much pain was in her. Her face was down but she managed to look up into my face. I was so confused, I did not know what to say, I tried to open my mouth but I was tong tight, then finally I said "all is well" and held her hand, then she leaned on my shoulder and though she said it so slowly and quietly, in hear tears I could hear her say "I should have known, I thought he was the one for me, I was a fool, I was so blind I could not see" I told her not to worry herself so much about Felix and that she was a beautiful girl and sooner enough she was going to find someone who would treat her better and even love her more, and she cried on my should this time a little bit loud saying that she hoped so.

As she cried, I embraced her, and held her in my arms like she was my baby. It killed me to see her cry, and I hated Felix for breaking my angel's heart. And finally in my arms she closed her eyes and fell asleep,

A few minutes after she had fallen asleep, I calmly took her hands off me and pulled over a pillow and laid her head, and then I calmly walked outside the door just to find Tracy and her fiancé kissing.

"I ca not imagine that's what you guys are doing when somebody is dying in there"

And Kevin replied

"We are just happy that type of a thing has not happened to us"

So I told them she had fallen asleep and that no one should wake her up. I told them it was good for her to take away some of the pain by sleeping.

Night came and Vanessa was still asleep, so Kevin carried her to my bed in my room and I spent the night in the couch. It was a cold night but it was worth it. I did it for Vanessa.

CHAPTER 18

The next morning Tracy got up very early and prepared breakfast, Kevin and I also got up earlier than Vanessa and we all wondered how we were going to face her when she woke up.

Then while we sat and ate breakfast, we heard the door open, and we saw her quietly walk towards the dining table. Kevin wanted to get up and run away into the kitchen but Tracy held him back.

Vanessa came and pulled over a chair and sat down without saying a word. Then Tracy said "good morning' and Vanessa replied good morning in a boring sorrowful way, and then Kevin and I said "good morning" together as if we were waiting for Vanessa to speak. Then out of curiosity I asked her "how did you sleep last night?" Kevin and Vanessa looked at me with bad eyes as if they were going to chew me raw. Then surprisingly Vanessa said, "Your room was a little bit nasty and scary but I was able to make it through the night" then smiles returned to the table but Tracy still warned me without letting Kevin or Vanessa Notice it.

Kevin started talking about his job interview which was coming up, but then Vanessa brought up the Felix topic which we had decided to avoid. Vanessa said she had been a fool to think that Felix was the right one for her. She said she knew it was going to take time but she was ready to get over him, and she begged us not to make her feel bad by feeling sorry for her.

As days passed she got better and I could see like magic how her swollen face got back to shape and how joy took back its place in her life. She became very close to me and for about a week she continued to stay with us till when Kevin passed his job interview.

We celebrated the event with joy and by that day I could tell that though Vanessa had not completely gotten over Felix, she was willing to move on with life. But there's a something I'm forgetting to mention. Kevin's job was in Kenya, and he was going to return to Yaoundé every two weeks to meet family and friends. It was the ideal job he had always wanted.

Tracy seemed very ok with that and Vanessa and I had no objection.

Vanessa finally went back to their house though she complained she felt so lonely over there and most of the times she would come hang around with Tracy and I.

As time passed, Vanessa and I became friends, we walked together and I loved it when I saw her happy. Being with her made me happy. Tracy and Kevin too were very happy to see that she was moving on and that she was happy and they often thanked me for helping her get out of her cage.

A few months later, Tracy and Kevin declared to us that they had decided on their wedding day and Vanessa and I were going to be the best lady and best man. We rejoiced over it, and anxiously waited for the wedding day. It was just two months away and we all started preparations.

CHAPTER 19

Two days before the church wedding, was the traditional wedding, which took place in Tiko village, where Tracy's grand parents lived. It was a long journey there, but yet a worthy and successful one. And I enjoyed observing their tradition. It was my first time in that part of the country and I was really amazed at the beauty of the place.

Finally came the wedding day. The day we all had been waiting for. I had always known I was going to be the best man at Kevin's wedding someday, and now the day had come. I wondered what Tracy was going to look like in her veil; I wondered what Vanessa felt like to be a best lady.

Its really exciting how time can pass so fast. Just yesterday we were kids playing with balloons and today we are all grown up, and ready to live with partners.

While Kevin and I dressed, he told me he was so anxious and I asked him to calm down. I looked at him and told him he looked hansom and happy. We both talked and laughed, till the moment came. The small church bell jingled, and the catechist moved into our dressing room and asked us to come out.

We came out of the room and walked down the red carpet to the alter. The church was full of family and friends and we both put our heads pointing straight to the alter to run away from any distractions. As we came in, the population stood up and we could perfectly hear the pianist play every single note of the popular wedding classic.

After the procession, we stood at the alter and faced the population this time with joy on our faces and even a fool would tell that it came from the heart. Then a second bell was jingled, and the church door was opened.

It was all white, and despite the fact that her veil covered her face, she looked extremely beautiful. The notes of the pianist fell on their steps, and four little beautiful girls threw red rose petals on the floor for them to walk on.

Vanessa walked behind Tracy and watched her long wedding gown from catching any obstacle. Tracy's wedding entrance was like in a fairy tale. For a second, I thought I was dreaming. Kevin could not stop smiling as they walked closer and closer to the alter.

Finally they arrived at the alter. Tracy stood facing Kevin, and Vanessa and I shifted a little bit down. I looked at Vanessa and quietly told her she looked gorgeous and she too quietly smiled and thanked me.

Kevin and Tracy made their vows and the priest declared them husband and wife. They kissed and before we knew it, we were already partying at the town hall where the after party took place.

That night, Tracy and her husband traveled to Kribi for their honeymoon and only returned a week later.

The next morning, Vanessa and I and a couple of family members and close friends cleaned around the house, and finally by the end of the day all of those to came over had gone back.

Kevin had long been preparing for his marriage life. He had already rented a new apartment in town for him and his wife. Which they were going to begin staying in immediately they returned from their honeymoon.

I knew life was going to be boring for me once Kevin was gone. It was time I got my self into a serious relationship. But I was still in the process of building my company. I had very big dreams of becoming the biggest business man in the continent. And I knew getting into a relationship with a woman at that time was not a very good step for my company.

But yet, the loneliness I felt in my heart was going to slowly kill me. I still loved Vanessa, but she was a no go section. It had been long since she broke up with Felix and she had already learned to live without him and happily for me, she had not yet picked up a new boyfriend. I still had a shot at her so I decided to start over again.

CHAPTER 20

I could no longer live in disguise, I was tired of hiding my love, and I was bored of behaving as if nothing was happening between us. I had held it so deep I was afraid keeping it inside my heart will kill me. So I decided to write a text message to Vanessa saying

"I am more determined than ever.
I believe you were meant for me.
I would never stop loving you.
Give me a call anytime you think am worth it,
Am always ready to receive you
Even if you come with your face pilled off
Even if you lose a leg
Even if you are a beast"

By next morning, I had not received any response from her and I guessed she had not seen my message so this time around I decided to call her. When I called, she picked up and I heard her voice say hello. I immediately asked her if she had seen my message, and she accepted and told me to forget about it. She reminded me that Kevin was going to personally tear me into pieces if he found out about it. But I told her I could not believe that of all things on earth, the one person I should fear so much was my best friend. I told her Kevin was my friend and if he truly loved me as a friend, he would give me his blessings.

Then she told me she had one condition for me. She told me she was going to accept my proposal, if and only if I told Kevin first.

I accepted the challenge like a big boy and I was very determined. We chatted over lots of other things happily. It felt like we were already going out together. Kevin and Tracy still had a few days before they'll return from their honeymoon.

The next day Vanessa visited me and we happily chatted. The more we talked the more I love her.

CHAPTER 21

Though she had not yet accepted me, I noticed a great difference in my relationship with her. We became normal friends and life returned to the way it was or maybe even better. She felt happier with me. We laughed and played together.

Vanessa called me almost everyday, and she started to care about me, she started caring about what I wore or said, she started giving me advise on what I could do to boost sales at my company, and last of all I noticed that she would now try to justify any action she made to me, if she visited a friend, she would tell me, if a friend visited her , she would tell me, if she was traveling, she would tell me and immediately she returned she would call me first. If she spent the night at a friends place she would tell me and try to explain to me that she did not mean to. She started behaving as if she owed me explanations, as if I were her husband.

Finally Kevin and Tracy returned, but their new home was a little bit far from where Vanessa and I lived. Vanessa and I visited them the day they returned, but that was not a good day to tell Kevin such a thing. I planned to tell him a few days later.

But unfortunately for me, Kevin traveled the next day for work and this time around he was going to spend not his usual two weeks but one month.

I wondered how lonely his wife would be and we talked about it. But from all indications Tracy was ok with it.

The next day after Kevin had traveled; Vanessa sent me a text message which read thus.

"You are a jerk, so you ca not even face Kevin and you claim to love me. From what I see you are not truly in love, because once in love we are always willing to do anything possible to have the one we love"

When I read the message I understood that Vanessa truly loved me. I felt more love in my heart than ever. So I decided to go to her house without informing her. I knocked at the door and when she opened, I could see her heart beat and I saw how much she loved me. It was all written over her face. She smiled and asked me to come in. I walked in and sat down and she offered me a glass of wine. Vanessa also sat down besides me and we talked about Tracy and Kevin.

Then, I decided to talk to her about us; I told her she could still accept me if truly she loved me, and together though the good and bad times we could make it through. She laughed and did not seem to really take me serious, but what I did not know was that I had planted just the seed I needed to plant.

Then like every desperate guy I tried my chance once more. I grabbed her by the hand and looked into her eyes, then in the softest way possible, I said to her "Vanessa you know I love you, and in case you do not know, I also know that you love me too, but what I do not understand is why you would let some stupid reasons come over us. I know you think the two of have no chances of lasting together forever, but for now that we both still have the opportunity to love and to have each other, lets not live to regret it. Let's make every single moment count. Before I go please accept me, I do not want much. Just a minute of your love and I will be satisfied for ever. If this is my one chance then just let me hold you in my arms, kiss you, and tell you I love you."

I knew she was a weak girl, and I saw her gradually falling for me. Then as I continued to speak, I moved closer to her, held her by the neck, and turned her face towards mine, looked into her eyes, passed my fingers over her hair. She did not resist, so I went forward and we kissed.

To my greatest surprise, as we kissed, she held me tight, and sucked my lips like she never ever wanted to let me go. In this moment I felt so alive, I wished it could last forever. For once in my life I received a kiss from true love. It felt like a dream, it felt like heaven on earth, it felt like magic.

I told her that I loved her and she said same to me, and again we kissed. Then we started laughing, and then she told me how much she has always loved me but was afraid that I was not going to love her back and that Kevin was not going to like us together.

So together with her, we promised never to break each others heart, and to stand by each other no matter what. We knew it was not going to be easy to affront Kevin but we were ready for what ever came our way.

That's the craziest thing about love. It makes even the wisest of all men, fools. It makes the strongest of all men, week. It makes us see possibilities in everything.

We talked a lot about many different things and I finally left her house a happy man that day.

CHAPTER 22

We knew Kevin still had sometime outside the country and we were not yet ready to tell Tracy. We wanted to tell the two of them at the same time.

The time we had before Kevin returned was very precious and sweet. We played together, ate together, talked together, and went to the movies together, kissed together, attended parties together. We did almost everything together.

The bond that held us together was so strong that not even a trailer would tear us apart.

As from the moment I started going out with Vanessa, I understood the meaning of love. I always thought nothing was worth dying for, but I realized love was worth it.

The people, who saw us together, enjoyed and encouraged it. They said we both really fitted together, and that indeed made us stronger.

We were so munch drunk in love that we forgot to take note of time, and to our greatest surprise, Kevin called and said he had arrived at was at home with his wife.

Vanessa panicked, but I asked her to be strong, and told her nothing was going to separate us as long as we were together.

We left and in a about thirty minutes we were already at their house, we greeted and chatted and ate and drank, as if nothing was wrong, but rather as if something was right. I remember Kevin mentioning that Vanessa and I seemed to be getting along so strong and we laughed over it, but none of us said anything.

It was just the first day he returned and telling him such a thing would mean killing his mood, so we decided to wait for a few more days.

Kevin was always very good at observing and drawing conclusions, I knew even if we did not tell him, he was going to realize it somehow, and that would be worse.

Kevin came on Tuesday and now it was Friday, Vanessa and I agreed to go tell Kevin and Tracy about our affair.

Honestly we had completely made up our minds to do so and face what ever consequences. Its funny how love is like hunger, it can make you do things you never dared to do.

When we arrived at their house, we saw them rejoicing, it was almost like a party for two till we arrived.

We joined them in rejoicing even before we asked why. Immediately I saw them rejoicing I knew it was a very bad time to tell what we wanted to say, so I signaled Vanessa not to make mention of it and congratulated them. It was really a happy evening

Kevin and Vanessa shared much to us about married life, as if they knew we were going out together. They said they could not wait for us to find our soul mates and they reminded us that we were not getting any older.

Finally we succeeded to get Kevin and Tracy to tell us why they were rejoicing so much and they said Tracy was pregnant. We rejoiced more with them when we heard the news. We did not want to spoil the good humor in the house with our own wahala, so we ended up not telling them about our affair.

We left their house very disappointed and I in person felt like a jerk. A real man always faces his problems directly and on time, only a coward would postpone or be afraid to face them.

CHAPTER 23

We promised ourselves we were not going to keep the secrete any longer. We went to visit Tracy and Kevin the next day, but they had visitors so we could not be able to tell them.

Ugly enough for us that was the case till Kevin finally left for work, so we had to wait for two weeks.

Please do not say we never tried, at least it was not our fault. Something always came up to prevent us from telling them.

First was the pregnancy news, next visitors and next either Kevin would be too busy or not in the mood and all those sorts of things. But I guess somehow he had started to notice our close relationship.

As for Tracy, she already started suspecting us, even from the way she looked at me; I could always tell there was something in her mind that she had to free out.

One perfect Friday morning, after Kevin had left, I stood out enjoying the fresh cold dry season morning breeze which brought me back to memories of when we were still very young and strong, I remembered all the dreams we had and I smiled as I could see them gradually coming to reality,

Then I heard my phone ring. It was Tracy, I wondered why she would be calling me that early in the morning, so I did not hesitate to pick.

She sounded normal and greeted me and said she would be very grateful if I passed by their house anytime I was free during the day, and I promised her I was going to pass by.

Throughout the day even as I sat in my office chair in my company which by the way was gradually growing up to my satisfaction, I wondered what Tracy wanted us to talk about. Something in me said it was about Vanessa and I, I became so impatient that I went to check on her at one o'clock.

When I arrived she had just finished preparing launch, and she invited me to join her on the table. We ate quietly and after eating and finishing my glass of wine, I asked her why she wanted to see me, then to funny enough she said she was just feeling lonely and thought talking to me could make her feel better.

I took that opportunity and we chatted and laughed, then I decided to confide on her about

Vanessa and I, and about how we were afraid to let them know especially Kevin.

First I asked her if I could trust her, and I asked her to promise to keep our discoursion as confidential as possible. She did promise me, so I told her I was completely in love with a girl who in turn loved me back very much, and we have been going out for sometime now. Tracy wanted to know the girls name and asked me to arrange a meeting with her, but I told her there was no need for that because she perfectly knew the girl. She told me she did not know any girl she could picture me with, I told her due to some reasons I was afraid to let her and her husband know of the girl because I was afraid they would not accept our relationship.

Tracy told me my choice was my choice and asked me "who are we to be against your choice, and by the way why would we?" so I told her, "actually the reason I or we have been hiding to let you know is because the girl in question is Vanessa"

"Which Vanessa are you talking about" Tracy asked, "how many Vanessas do you know?" I replied. Then she said "o my God" and locked her mouth with her hands and looked surprised. Then she said "Do you know that Kevin is going to skin you alive if he hears this?" "That's exactly why we have been hiding it" I said. Then Tracy laughed for a while and asked me if I was very sure about what I had just told her, and I said yes. She asked if I was very sure that Vanessa loved me and that we had been going out for sometime in secrete and I confirmed.

Before I knew it we were already smiling and I was telling Vanessa how much I loved Vanessa and how I wanted to marry her. She once more asked me if I was sure Vanessa felt same for me as I did for her. And I affirmatively answered.

Tracy looked amazed and I was surprised when she said she was happy for me because I had finally I had found true love. She said she thought I was never going to find true love so easy. Then I told her it was not so easy. Because I still had to face my best friend who as you know was her husband.

CHAPTER 24

Tracy picked up her phone from the couch and said she wanted to make a call. She dialed the number and walked into the room. Then I saw her walk out with a great smile on her face.

"She is coming over here right away" Tracy said and immediately I knew she was talking about my girl friend Vanessa who in other words was her best friend and her husband's junior sister.

Tracy and I kept on chatting for about three minutes before Vanessa finally arrived. Once Vanessa opened the door, Tracy started talking to her.

"I thought you were my best friend

I shared all my secrets with you but yet you did not do same to me. I am so disappointed with you. Shame on you honey," Vanessa did not seem to understand where Tracy was driving to because she had not yet seen me sitting on the couch.

"Girl, what on earth are you talking about" Vanessa replied. Then I looked back and she saw me and the look on my face, and she looked surprised. She was tong tide.

"Oh my God!

Jackson!

I ca not believe you told her, I am disappointed in you, now Kevin is going to know and tear us into pieces."

"Honey I am sorry I should have told you before letting Tracy know but I did not plan to tell her" I replied. Then I tried to convince her that I did not mean to tell Tracy about it and that I was sorry for betraying her.

Then I heard Tracy say that I had no reason to be sorry, Tracy asked Vanessa to calm down and said.

"Vanessa, Honey,

The reason I called you over here was just to let you know that I am happy for you and that I will always stand by you no matter what."

Then I heard Vanessa say "O my God" this time with a happy tone. She was excited, I too was happy, we embraced Tracy and thanked her. Vanessa and I embraced ourselves and kissed and Tracy was like WOW!

It was like we were still high school, we talked and laughed and played with Tracy. Tracy how ever due to her condition did not jump a lot. One could actually start seeing the stomach look bigger than usual.

Tracy sat down and asked us to sit down with her. She looked tired, and held her back like all pregnant women would do. Then she asked us to tell her all the story. She asked us to tell her when we started and how me managed to keep this secrete all this time.

We told her our story and told her how we had tried to let them know, and how something always got in our way. Tracy looked at us as if she had just seen a romance movie. She became our fan, and we were the stars.

But then our faces saddened when we thought and talked about how we were going to let Kevin know.

"Now Kevin is going to consider me as part of your conspiracy, but all the same I am going to stand by you" Tracy said and we held our hands together hoping for the best.

Kevin was not going to return so early so we had enough time to plan on how to approach him. But one thing was certain. The earlier we approached him the better for us.

Before Vanessa and I left Tracy, we decided we were going to let Kevin know the same day he was going to return from Europe. I was against that because I knew he always looked very tired the day he returned, especially after the long flight.

CHAPTER 25

Time passed so fast and by Wednesday Kevin informed he was returning on Friday. We prayed for the days coming that all should work out well. We knew it was not an easy task, but we were ready for it.

Friday came and Kevin arrived. Tracy called us and said Kevin was home. She asked us to come over, and reminded us that we were going to let him know and told us not to be afraid; she promised once more to stand by us.

It was already 4 PM that Friday, and the sun was gradually dying down. I must confess Vanessa looked very beautiful that day and for once in my life I felt lucky. I looked at her and thanked God for giving me the woman of my dreams.

Before we left my house, we looked at each other like it was our last moment together.

It took us just three minutes to get to Kevin's house. We packed the par outside the gate, and walked in.

Vanessa was so nervous and anxious and I could see fear written all over her face. So before I knocked the door, I decided that we talk a little bit.

I told her all was going to be well and reminded her that Vanessa was going to support us. We both were scared of the unknown and so to reduce our fear and to feel save, we decided to kiss.

I held her very tight by the left hand, and then she places her right hand on my left chest directly where my heart was. My heart beat so much faster and then we both kissed over and over again.

The door opened without us noticing, we were lost in each others lips. Then we heard a fake male cough, by the door. That is just when we realized that the door had been opened. It was Kevin. He had seen us.

We all looked at him so surprised and ashamed and weak. Vanessa started crying, without saying a word. Kevin too looked at us for a moment without saying anything, and then walked in to the house.

That feeling of betrayal killed my spirit, we wondered if we should go into the house, stand outside or walk away. Then Tracy came out and asked us to come in.

We walked into the house with her, and I told her all that had happened. Kevin had walked into the room and we sat outside at the sitting room wondering how we were going to approach him.

Tracy kept telling us to have faith, and reminded us that the love was ours and the decision was ours and not that of Kevin or any other person.

Then Kevin walked out of the room, his face looked like that of a hungry angry lion in the jungle. I had never seen him look that before.

I wondered what he was going to do to me. I wondered what I was going to tell him, I could not help thinking about what was going on, in Vanessa's brain.

Tracy stood up and walked towards Kevin, saying, "honey its not exactly what you are thinking. They have been planning on telling you about it, and they even confided on me, they were afraid to affront you." But then he just pushed her aside and called all three of us pretenders.

Kevin asked the two of us to leave his house and never to come by again. He told me I had betrayed him and hence I was no longer his best friend. He said as for Vanessa, he was still thinking about what to do, but he was really disappointed with her. I tried to apologize to Kevin and he seemed to listen till I worsened things by saying that I honestly and truly loved Vanessa and that I was sorry because nothing on earth could ever make me stop loving her.

Kevin insisted and we finally left the house. Tracy advised us to leave so that he may calm down, and told us that she was going to talk with him and give us feedback.

We had no other option than to leave. I knew deep down that time was going to play its role and that with time Kevin was going to start to understand. I expected him to understand this better than me.

As we walked out the door, I looked back, and then I said my last words to Kevin. "Thank you" I said.

Kevin looked at me and replied "traitor". Then Vanessa and I held each other by the hand and found our way out the gate into the car. We spoke no words to each other and I kept on wondering how Vanessa had managed to say nothing to Kevin.

Was it the fear, or was it reason. That preoccupied my brain till we arrived at my place. I asked Vanessa to stay because she was really exhausted, and especially because we both needed each other at that moment more than ever.

CHAPTER 26

I did not feel any pain till I went to bed. I could not sleep. I could not help remembering how Kevin and I had grown up together. We had always been honest to each other. I thought about how much we loved each other and how long we had come.

Twenty eight years together was not a small thing, I could not just let it go like that.

But then on the other hand was Vanessa. I felt more love for her than ever. I was going to spend the rest of my life with her. Though we had only been in love for a short time as compared to the time I had spent with Kevin. The bond between us was stronger.

Between my lover and my best friend, who was I going to chose? It was not really a question I could be asking at the moment because before God and man and in any situation I would still choose Vanessa over Kevin.

I wanted both of them, but I could only have one. Vanessa and I never really talked about it that night. But by next day morning, we both felt a little better.

If it was not for that kiss maybe Kevin would have treated us better. Vanessa was so angry with Kevin that she actually decided she was not going to try any further to ask him to accept us together. She was my choice so I supported her decision.

We never ever visited Kevin again, Tracy often called and we chatted and sometimes she visited us. We had nothing to fear for any longer so Vanessa packed all her things and moved over to my house. We were very happy together.

Tracy kept on trying to talk to Kevin about it but he often closed the topic even before she began. He truly felt betrayed as to what Tracy told us.

Kevin finally traveled back to Europe for work and spent 2 months away this time. Vanessa and I had learned to put Kevin aside and face our future together but deep in our hearts it still killed us.

For me, he was my best friend and I felt so wrong for betraying him but I had no choice.

For Vanessa he was her bother. Honestly it was very difficult to live with all those thoughts.

Two months passed and Kevin returned. Tracy told us he had returned, but we did not seem very interested in his coming till one day we heard the knock on the door.

Before we heard the knock on the door we were lying on the carpet together eating pop corn and watching some love romantic Indian movie. I reduced the volume level and asked Vanessa to go check out who it was.

She walked to the door and opened it. And then I heard her call me to come over. I thought maybe it was the mailman or maybe the electrician or plumber, but to my greatest surprise I saw Tracy and her husband. Vanessa had her hands all over the door like she never wanted them to get in.

I came closer and looked at Kevin quietly and asked Vanessa to let them come in.

They walked in and I could see Kevin pass his eyes all over the house. He had not visited me since he got married. Tracy seemed to look happy and felt so free.

We offered them juice, and then I asked if they had come to the neighborhood and decided to pass by to say hi. But Tracy said they had come but to see us. Vanessa said "I thought your husband had declared us non grata" then Tracy replied "please do not say that"

Kevin was so quiet all through till he finally spoke his first words. He looked sad and weak when he spoke. I could tell what he was saying came directly from his heart.

"I know you guys are wondering what I am doing here. I know you do not want me here, but I just came to tell you guys that I am very sorry. Please do find it in your heart to forgive me. I was wrong, and I've realized my errors. I should have accepted the fact that my best friend could date my junior sister. I should have supported you people, i am very ashamed I deserted and disowned you even when you needed me most. Words may not really be able to explain but I am sorry. I just want you to forgive even if you woo not take me back."

We were all quiet for sometime after Kevin stopped apologizing. I looked at Vanessa and she looked at me, and we both smiled from our hearts then I spoke out to Kevin

"No Kevin, you should not be sorry, you just did what every elder brother and best friend would do. We do not blame you in any way nor do we hold any crush against you. Rather we should be the ones to beg for your forgiveness and blessing, because we betrayed you."

Then Tracy said "big bro, I am sorry for falling in love with your best friend, but it is not my doing, it the work of God"

Then Tracy said "oo girl, come over here," and Vanessa moved towards her and they embraced, then Kevin too joined them and embraced and then Tracy called me over and joined them.

CHAPTER 27

For once again, the fantastic four were back together, the atmosphere was full of love. Just a hug and we put away all the sad memories of the past and were ready to welcome a new future.

Kevin confessed to us that he had truly seen that Vanessa and I loved each other very much and that he never ever wanted to be blamed for separating us. We laughed over it, and popped a bottle of Champaign and toasted to our renewed friendship. Kevin told us he was going to stand by us, and asked us to always call on him anytime we needed anything. Then Kevin and I chatted about his job and about my company. We both were amazed on how far each of us had gone to achieve our dreams and we were happy with it. The girls too chatted alone but we could not know what they chatted about.

It was a happy moment and any idea to make the moment happier was welcomed. So I brought out another bottle of Champaign and popped it. But before I popped it, I reached my hand into my pocket. The three looked at me like "what the hell does he want to do" then I asked them to pay attention to me for a moment. Then I said;

“I have always wanted to do this

But the environment did not permit me to

But now that we are all happy here tonight

Tracy I must thank you for being by our side throughout this moments of temptation.

Kevin I am happy you were able to accept us; we have come a long way.

Vanessa, you know I love you beyond all doubt, and luckily for me you too love me back. With Tracy and Kevin as my witnesses, nothing would be sweeter than cementing this relationship which we already have.” Then I brought out the shining golden ring from my pocket, looked at Vanessa and said

“This is not actually how I planned to do this, but Vanessa Will you marry me?”

Tracy looked at Vanessa, and Kevin too looked at her. She smiled, and looked at me, but did not make a move, and then I went down on my knees, and said “pleeeeeeeeeeeese” and then she stood up walked towards me, and said “with all pleasure” then I put the ring in her finger, and we embraced and kissed.

Tracy and Kevin felt touched. And the embraced themselves as if it were their engagement day. I felt so complete. I carried Vanessa up and we danced to the music. Then I popped the bottle I had been holding. It was like the party for four had just begun.

Kevin walked towards me, congratulated me and told me he was happy for me.

It was getting very late and so our visitors decided to leave. We accompanied them to their car, and happy parted and waved as they left.

When they left, we rejoiced over and over again. That was one of the sweetest days of my life. I kept on embracing, carrying and kissing Vanessa. I thanked her for accepting to marry me. I had never seen Vanessa look so happy. She felt relieved; she told me she thought I was never going to ask her to marry me.

We planned our wedding day, and made sure we chose a day when Kevin would be available. We had three months to get married. I could not help but dream of the day when Vanessa and I would finally be declared husband and wife. Kevin was going to be our best man and Tracy was going to be the bride's mate but she rejected though she said she loved to but feared that she might be in labor by that time or maybe in the hospital after giving birth. She expected her baby about that time.

CHAPTER 28

The wedding day came so fast. I could not understand how those three months had succeeded to pass so fast. We invited family and friends, and they all looked so happy to see us get married. Most of them were surprised that Vanessa and I were getting married but they loved it.

That Saturday, I stood at the alter, with Kevin at my back, and I watched the angel walk down the isle towards me. She was all in white and glittered like gold. She looked like a creature from heaven; I counted myself amongst the luckiest of all men to finally be getting married to a princess like her.

When I pulled the veil over her head, I was shocked at the beauty, her lips were perfect, her cheeks were sparkling, and her eyes glowed like a lamb when she smiled.

Kevin looked at me and smiled, we kissed and the crowd cheered. We had just been declared husband and wife. The choir sang songs that echoed up to the heavens and the people gave us their blessings and we walked out together. While we stood outside taking pictures, Tracy walked up to me and said, ": the baby kicked in my stomach when you kissed" and I told her that was a blessing.

The after party was indeed splendid, with lots of food and drink for everybody. We rejoiced and celebrated together. And then evening came and my wife and I left for our one week honeymoon to Kenya. We have always talked about it. We had always wanted to go there, especially how Kevin had worked there. To see the Beatifull Mountains, birds, elephants and wide wild forest creatures. We enjoyed being in Kenya till we finally returned.

When we returned from honeymoon, we decided to visit Kevin and his wife. To our greatest surprise, Tracy and her husband had become parents. 'Tracy gave birth to Tatiana the next day after your wedding" Kevin said.

It was amazing to see Tracy finally become a mother. We congratulated them, and I could see the look on Adel's face, when she carried Tatiana in her arms and As I joke I told her "don't worry honey, we will soon start making our own babies" and we all laughed. Kevin felt so lucky. He indeed was happy and I too was happy for him.

That's exactly why we were crying, that's exactly why there was sorrow all over the place. That exactly why Tracy felt like killing herself. How could this happen to us. We all were meant to be together. We should have told him not to leave. At least he would have lived.

The fantastic four had been broken and only memories were left. I am talking about Kevin's accident, I am talking about the fact that he died. I am talking about the fact that he did not live to see his baby grow. She was only two months for Gods sake.

You never know love till you've lost someone you loved. I know it is going to be hard for us, but where there is life there is always a way. Life will have to move on; goodbye was all we had to say, though as we watched him leave it killed us inside.

The last words he said was that he would be back before we knew it. But I guess he lied. No. he said the truth, it is just that he returned in a way we did not expect. He returned in a wooden box called a coffin. He was gone. Gone to rise no more.

This is how it all happened. Kevin had requested a two month leave from work before coming for our wedding. And when those two months were over he left for work. He never finally even reached the airport. We just saw it on the news.

The car he was in was hit by a truck, and both he and his colleague died on the spot.

CHAPTER 29

Agnes was of great help to us. She really played her role. She knew the job of a bride's mate never always only ended at the alter. Although she may never be able to replace Kevin. She has come to gain a great position in our hearts.

She was there for us when we lost all hope and she helped us to get over the loss.

I have always acted as Tatiana's father and will continue to do.

Tracy has now though it was difficult, gotten over her lost husband, but I don't think she will be able to remarry again. She hates when I bring up the topic

As for my sweetheart and I, we are already at our number three which may be the last. I named the first one Kevin after Kevin my best friend and the next two, Adel and Frederick.

My business is doing fine and I am gradually becoming rich, famous and influential as I have always wished to be. My wife is living proof of the saying that by every successful man is always a woman. Love indeed is a strong bond. Thought our moments of trials and temptations may come and go. The love between us always has its way.

www.ingramcontent.com/pod-product-compliance
Ingram Content Group UK Ltd.
Pitfield, Milton Keynes, MK11 3LW, UK
UKHW020219250726
13967UKWH00001B/89

9 781105 806612